The 4th of July

Dorothy Goeller

Bailey Books
an imprint of
Enslow Publishers, Inc.
40 Industrial Road
Box 398
Berkeley Heights, NJ 07922
USA
http://www.enslow.com

Bailey Books, an imprint of Enslow Publishers, Inc.

Library of Congress Cataloging-in-Publication Data

Goeller, Dorothy.
The 4th of July / Dorothy Goeller.
p. cm. — (All about holidays)
 Includes index.
Summary: "Simple text and photographs present a story with a 4th of July theme"—
Provided by publisher.
ISBN 978-0-7660-3806-6
1. Fourth of July—Juvenile literature. I. Title. II. Title: The Fourth of July.
E286.A1282 2011
394.2634—dc22   2010013462
Paperback ISBN: 978-1-59845-175-7

Printed in the United States of America

062010 Lake Book Manufacturing, Inc., Melrose Park, IL

10 9 8 7 6 5 4 3 2 1

To Our Readers: We have done our best to make sure all Internet Addresses in this book
were active and appropriate when we went to press. However, the author and the publisher
have no control over and assume no liability for the material available on those Internet sites
or on other Web sites they may link to. Any comments or suggestions can be sent by e-mail
to comments@enslow.com or to the address on the back cover.

✪ Enslow Publishers, Inc., is committed to printing our books on recycled paper. The paper
in every book contains 10% to 30% post-consumer waste (PCW). The cover board on the
outside of each book contains 100% PCW. Our goal is to do our part to help young people
and the environment too!

Photo Credits: U.S. Navy photo by Chief Photographer's Mate Chris Desmond, p. 4, U. S.
Navy photo by Mass Communications Specialist 1st Class Mark O'Donald, p. 10; All others
Shutterstock, com.

Cover Photo: Shutterstock.com.

Note to Parents and Teachers
Help pre-readers get a jumpstart on reading. These lively stories introduce simple concepts
with repetition of words and short simple sentences. Photos and illustrations fill the pages
with color and effectively enhance the text. Free Educator Guides are available for this
series at www.enslow.com. Search for the *All About Holidays* series name.

Contents

Words to Know

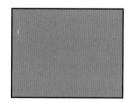  

blue   flag   red

The colors of our flag

Red, white, and blue

8

Red, white, and blue

Colors of our flag

Colors of our flag

Soon it will be
the 4th of July.

And that, you know, is why we sing.

We sing about our country's flag.

Red, white, and blue

Happy 4th of July to you!

Read More

Marx, David F., *Independence Day.* Danbury, Conn.: Children's Press, 2001.

Nelson, Robin, *Independence Day.* Minneapolis, Minn.: Lerner Books, 2003.

Web Sites

Enchanted Learning's Crafts. *Activities and Crafts for July 4th.* <http://www.enchantedlearning.com/crafts/july4/>

Kaboose. *Fourth of July Coloring Pages.* <http://holidays.kaboose.com/july4-color.html>

Index

Guided Reading Level: **B**
Guided Reading Leveling System is based on the guidelines recommended by Fountas and Pinnell.

Word Count: 48